I'm Going To READ!™

These levels are meant only as guides;
you and your child can best choose a book that's right.

Level 1: Kindergarten–Grade 1 . . . Ages 4–6
- word bank to highlight new words
- consistent placement of text to promote readability
- easy words and phrases
- simple sentences build to make simple stories
- art and design help new readers decode text

Level 2: Grade 1 . . . Ages 6–7
- word bank to highlight new words
- rhyming texts introduced
- more difficult words, but vocabulary is still limited
- longer sentences and longer stories
- designed for easy readability

Level 3: Grade 2 . . . Ages 7–8
- richer vocabulary of up to 200 different words
- varied sentence structure
- high-interest stories with longer plots
- designed to promote independent reading

Level 4: Grades 3 and up . . . Ages 8 and up
- richer vocabulary of more than 300 different words
- short chapters, multiple stories, or poems
- more complex plots for the newly independent reader
- emphasis on reading for meaning

LEVEL 2

Library of Congress Cataloging-in-Publication Data Available

2   4   6   8   10   9   7   5   3   1

Published by Sterling Publishing Co., Inc.
387 Park Avenue South, New York, NY 10016
Text copyright © 2005 by Harriet Ziefert Inc.
Illustrations copyright © 2005 by Richard Rossi
Distributed in Canada by Sterling Publishing
c/o Canadian Manda Group, 165 Dufferin Street
Toronto, Ontario, Canada M6K 3H6
Distributed in Great Britain and Europe by Chris Lloyd at Orca Book
Services, Stanley House, Fleets Lane, Poole BH15 3AJ, England
Distributed in Australia by Capricorn Link (Australia) Pty. Ltd.
P.O. Box 704, Windsor, NSW 2756, Australia

I'm Going To Read is a trademark of Sterling Publishing Co., Inc.

Sterling ISBN 1-4027-2720-8

Pillow Fight

Pictures by Richard Rossi

Sterling Publishing Co., Inc.
New York

**Mike and Tony
were buddies.**

**They walked to
school together.**

They ate lunch together.

**Mike picked Tony
for his team.**

And Tony picked Mike.

**After school
they played ball . . .**

and tag . . .

and leapfrog.

Sometimes they rode bikes.

**And sometimes they did
nothing much at all.**

On Friday nights Mike and Tony had sleepovers.

They took turns getting cookies.

**They took turns calling
their friends.**

**One Friday night Mike and Tony
had a pillow fight.**

**It was a small pillow
fight that grew . . .**

and grew . . .

and grew!

Mike and Tony threw down their pillows.

They grabbed each other.
Mike sat on Tony.

And Tony sat on Mike.
Tony yelled, "I win!"

**Mike shouted, "You did not!
You cheated!"**

**Mike took his sleeping bag
and ran out the door.**

find   go   said   him   let's

**Tony called his mother.
"Mike ran away!"**

"Let's go find him,"
said Tony's mother.

When Tony found Mike,
Mike yelled, "You didn't win!"

"Okay! Okay!" said Tony.
"I didn't win. Nobody did."

**Mike and Tony
were buddies again.**